Curious George
Goes to a Chocolate Factory

This Classic Book
Belongs To:

_____

MARGRET & H.A. REY'S
Curious George
Goes to a Chocolate Factory

Illustrated in the style of H. A. Rey by Vipah Interactive

Houghton Mifflin Harcourt

Boston   New York

Copyright © 1998 by Houghton Mifflin Harcourt Publishing Company

Based on the character of Curious George®, created by Margret and H. A. Rey.
Illustrated by Vipah Interactive: C. Becker, D. Fakkel, M. Jensen, S. SanGiacomo, C. Yu.

Curious George® and related characters, created by Margret and H. A. Rey, are copyrighted
and trademarked by Houghton Mifflin Harcourt Publishing Company and are used under license.

www.hmhco.com

The text of this book is set in Adobe Garamond.
The illustrations are watercolor.

This special edition was printed for Kohl's Department Stores, Inc. (for distribution on
behalf of Kohl's Cares, LLC, its wholly owned subsidiary) by Houghton Mifflin Harcourt
Publishing Company.

ISBN: 978-0-544-92094-1

Manufactured in China
SCP 10 9 8 7 6 5 4 3 2 1

Kohl's
Style #: 978-0-544-92094-1
Factory #: 123386
Manufactured Date: 7/16

This is George.

George was a good little monkey and always very curious.

One day George went for a drive with his friend, the man with the yellow hat.

"Look, George," the man said. "There's a store in that chocolate factory up ahead. Let's stop for a treat."

George loved chocolates.
Inside the store, boxes of
chocolates were stacked everywhere,
but the man with the yellow hat
found his favorites right away.
"George," he said, "wait here while
I buy these, and please stay out
of trouble."

George looked around the store.
He saw chocolate-covered cherries
and fudge-flavored lollipops.
A chocolate bunny caught his eye.

Then something else caught his eye.
What were all those people looking at?
George was curious.

He climbed up to get
a better look. Through
the window he saw lots
of trays filled with little
brown dots.

What were all those
little brown dots?

George was curious.
He found a door that led
to the other side of the window.

The little brown dots were chocolates, of course! A tour guide was showing a group of people how to tell what was inside the chocolates by looking at the swirls on top.

This little swirl means fudge,

this one says that caramel is inside,

and this wiggle is for marshmallow.

This is the squiggle for a truffle,

this one is for nougat,

this sideways swirl is for orange fluff,

and this one is for George's favorite — banana cream.

George followed the tour group until they came to a balcony
overlooking a room where the chocolates were made. Down below,
busy workers picked the candy off the machines and put them in boxes.

16

These were the machines that made the chocolates with the swirls on top! The chocolates came out of the machines on long belts. But how did they get their swirls?

George was curious.

He climbed down from the balcony . . .

and up onto a machine.

George peeked inside.
He was trying to see what
was making the swirls when
all of a sudden . . .

the chocolates began
coming out faster and
faster! They sped by him
so quickly they seemed
to be running on legs
of their own.

"Quick! Bring more boxes!" yelled a man with a tall white hat.

"What happened?" asked another man.

Nobody answered. Nobody knew what had happened and everyone was so busy that no one noticed George.

The workers began to fall behind and the candy began to fall off the end of the belt.

"Save the chocolates!" yelled the man with the tall white hat.

Meanwhile, George saw one of his favorites
whiz by. He tried to catch the banana-cream
chocolate, but it was too fast!

He chased it to the end of the belt.

At the end of the belt a pile of chocolates was growing taller and taller. George had never seen so many chocolates!

As he searched for the banana cream, he put the others in empty boxes.

George was a fast worker. Someone noticed and yelled, "Bring that monkey more boxes! He's helping us catch up!"

Not all the chocolates made it into boxes, but no more chocolates fell on the floor.

Just when George and the workers were all caught up, the tour guide ran in with the man with the yellow hat. "Get that monkey out of here!" she yelled. "He's ruining our chocolates!"

"But this little monkey SAVED the chocolates," explained the workers.

Then the man with the tall white hat said to George, "You may
have caused us some trouble, but you were a speedy little monkey.
You deserve a big box of candy for all your help."

George was glad he was not in trouble, but he did not take
the chocolates.

Back in the parking lot, the workers waved good-bye as George and his friend got into their little blue car.

"George, are you sure you don't want any chocolates before we leave?" asked the man with the yellow hat.

George was sure.